FOOTBALL
AUSTRALIA
PRESENTS

FOOTBALL FEVER

FOOTBALL FEVER

GALA DAY

KRISTIN DARELL

ILLUSTRATIONS BY LESLEY VAMOS

PUFFIN BOOKS

PUFFIN BOOKS

UK | USA | Canada | Ireland | Australia
India | New Zealand | South Africa | China

Penguin Random House Australia is part of the Penguin Random House group of companies whose addresses can be found at global.penguinrandomhouse.com.

First published by Puffin Books, an imprint of Penguin Random House Australia Pty Ltd, in 2023

Cover design by Caroline Lee © Penguin Random House Australia Pty Ltd
Illustrations by Lesley Vamos
Internal design and typesetting by Midland Typesetters, Australia

Printed and bound in Australia by Griffin Press, an accredited ISO AS/NZS 14001 Environmental Management Systems printer

A catalogue record for this book is available from the National Library of Australia

ISBN 978 1 76 104809 8

penguin.com.au

We at Penguin Random House Australia acknowledge that Aboriginal and Torres Strait Islander peoples are the Traditional Custodians and the first storytellers of the lands on which we live and work. We honour Aboriginal and Torres Strait Islander peoples' continuous connection to Country, waters, skies and communities. We celebrate Aboriginal and Torres Strait Islander stories, traditions and living cultures; and we pay our respects to Elders past and present.

CHAPTER 1

'What do you think, Harper?'

'Huh?' Harper pushed back her glasses and blinked, bringing the faces of her Merridale Fever U11s teammates back into focus. 'Sorry.' A sheepish grin spread across her face. 'I wasn't paying attention.'

'That's all good,' Crabbie said, laughing. 'I was asking if anyone had any ideas about how to beat Newhurst FC this year. I don't think I can stand *another* draw.'

It was Thursday training in the last week

of the club season. Newhurst FC was the only team other than the Fever that hadn't lost a game.

Sasha shrugged. 'I guess we just hope they play fair this time.'

'Yeah,' Finn replied, twisting his hair into a bun. 'Fat chance.'

'Two minutes,' Coach called out. 'Let's get moving.'

'I know Newhurst can be a bit rough, but they're not *all* bad,' Harper said.

'I love how you always see the best in people.' Meili smiled. 'What would we do without you?'

Harper laughed as Kyra raced in and grabbed Meili's hand.

'Let's not keep Mum – I mean Coach – waiting,' Kyra said, dragging her best friend onto the pitch. The others started heading out too.

‘Coming, Harper?’ Sasha asked.

‘I’ll be there in a sec.’ Harper crouched down and fiddled with her bag.

What would we do without you?

She swallowed against a lump in her throat. If everything went according to her parents’ plan, in three weeks, the team would find out *exactly* what they would do without her. Harper would be gone – living in a new home in the country, playing with a new football club. The only thing not set yet was her school. That depended on whether she got a football scholarship. She hadn’t told her Fever friends. She couldn’t. Not yet. There was only this game and Gala Day left. She didn’t want anything to change.

Harper took a deep breath, put a smile on her face and jogged over to her team. Coach was staring at the car park, her forehead wrinkled with concern.

‘Has anyone heard from Hani?’ Coach asked. ‘It’s not like him to be late, especially for the last training session.’

‘He was at school,’ Sasha said. She was in Hani’s class at Stickford Public School. Harper nodded. She went there as well. She’d seen him after lunch.

‘Hmm. I’m sure he’ll be here soon,’ Coach said. She turned to the team as a grin spread across her face. ‘It may be our last training session but that doesn’t mean we’re taking it easy. Kat, you know the drill. Jogging up and back. Let’s go.’

The lump was back in Harper’s throat as she watched her teammates head off one by one. Even Kyra’s golden retriever Diego joined in the warm-up. The team had barely changed since the Under 8s.

The lump turned into a giggle as she realised that if you looked at hair colour, the line her teammates were in made a pattern. Crabbie's red hair was first, then it alternated dark and light: Kat (dark), Ava (light) and Sam (dark). Kyra, Meili, Charlie, Sasha and Finn kept the pattern going. She was the odd one on the end, doubling up light-coloured hair with Finn. Hani's dark hair would have fitted perfectly between them, but he still hadn't arrived. With a final glance towards the car park, Harper joined the back of the line.

'Great work,' Coach said when they'd regrouped at the starting cone. 'Now laps of side shuffles, criss-crosses, fast feet and butt kickers. Then, Charlie, please take everyone through a stretch. I'm going to set up your first activity.'

Harper's mood lifted as the blood pumped faster around her body. By the time they'd finished stretching she was feeling much happier.

'Okay, everyone,' Coach said, waving them over. She'd placed eleven cones in a circle. 'It's Thursday, which means it's . . .'

'Quiz time!' they all called out.

'And as usual,' Coach continued, 'there's a slushie up for grabs.'

'Oh, Hani's going to be seriously bummed,' Crabbie said, chuckling.

Hani was the team's football encyclopedia. He'd won almost every Thursday slushie and had a large pile of vouchers saved up to show for it. Harper ran her hand through her short hair and squinted into the distance. Still no sign of her friend.

'This is a drill we haven't done in a while,' Coach explained. 'The set-up should be a clue. Any ideas?'

Ava's hand shot up. Coach nodded her way.

'I love this one,' Ava said. 'When you say, "two left", we all move two cones to the left. If you say, "three right, one left", we go that many cones right and left as well. If you say, "centre", we run to the middle and back.'

'Excellent,' Coach said, nodding. 'Now for a bonus extra slushie, can you tell me why we do this exercise?'

Ava's smile was huge. 'It's all about reaction time. We need to pay attention and move fast.'

'You got it.'

Kat gave Ava a high-five.

'Right. Let's start with side steps,' Coach said. 'Three left.'

Harper loved this drill too. There was no time to think of anything but where to move.

'Two right. Centre. One left,' Coach called out.

Harper spotted a flash of white fur dart into the circle between Finn and Sasha. Sasha's armed cartwheeled as she narrowly avoided ending up on the grass.

'Wrong way, Diego,' Finn said. Everyone laughed.

There were a lot of red cheeks by the time Coach ended the drill. Harper was about to grab a sip of water when she spotted something out of the corner of her eye.

Finally.

A familiar red car was pulling into the car park.

'Coach, Hani's here,' Harper said, her grin wide.

The door opened and Hani twisted out of the passenger seat.

Harper's smile faded. *Oh no!*

CHAPTER 2

His mum wanted him to rest, but Hani wasn't going to miss the last training of the season for anything – not even a busted knee. His teammates had been doing a circle drill. Now they were all frozen, staring at him. The range of expressions would have been funny if it wasn't for the reason why.

Harper was the first to move, racing towards him. She was his midfield partner on the pitch. They were an odd pair to look at – she only reached his shoulder in height and her hair was as fair as his was dark – but she was his closest friend in the team and she had an enormous heart.

'Oh Hani,' Harper said, her eyes wide. 'What happened?'

Hani shrugged. 'I twisted it and might have torn something. The meniscus, I think they called it. They also said something about the bit under my kneecap not being the normal shape.'

Harper winced. 'Does it hurt?'

'Not really. They gave me some stuff at the hospital.'

'Are you staying?' she asked.

He nodded. As he adjusted his crutches his lips pressed together and he forced a small smile. 'I can't miss our last training.'

He could see worry in Harper's eyes, but she just nodded. Hani was glad. He was disappointed enough. He didn't want a fuss.

‘Goodness me,’ Coach said, walking over. ‘This looks like a bit of bad luck.’

‘Hello.’ Hani’s mum joined them in front of the car. ‘Coach, a quick word?’

‘Of course,’ Coach said. ‘Why don’t you kids head over to the team. I’ll be there in a sec.’

Hani gave his mum a quick hug.

‘Please be careful,’ she said.

He rolled his eyes. ‘Yes, Mum.’

Hani could see the rest of his Fever teammates gathered near their bags and bottles. He was still a few metres away when the questions started. Everyone spoke at once.

‘Chill, guys,’ he said. ‘It’s totally boring. I was helping my little sister practise some football tricks. I put my foot down wrong and . . .’ Hani shrugged again.

‘Oof,’ Crabbie said. ‘Is it broken?’

'Nah.' Hani shrugged. 'But they won't let me play this week. They want to check some more stuff.'

'How long are you on those?' Finn asked, pointing at the crutches.

Hani shrugged again. 'Couple of days, maybe. Hopefully less. I can't miss Gala Day.'

His teammates were silent.

'Ava's already won the quiz slushie,' Harper said, eventually.

Hani looked at his friend, grateful. Then his eyes narrowed. 'Well, I suppose it's only fair that someone else gets at least one,' he said.

'Actually, I won two!' Ava grinned at him.

His teammates were laughing as Coach walked over.

'That really is bad luck, Hani,' she said. 'Hopefully the tests will give you the all clear and you'll be back running in no time. Until then, how about you help me out – be my assistant coach.'

Hani's chest felt tight.

I'm a player, he thought. *I don't want to coach.*

'Um, thanks,' he said. 'But I think I might just sit and watch. I'm feeling a bit funny.'

'Of course,' Coach said. 'The rest of you, we need two goals set up. We're going to work on formations.' She clapped. 'Let's move!'

As his Fever teammates flew into action, he saw Harper hesitate.

Hani smiled and shooed her away. Once he was sure she was distracted, he let his face drop. He *was* feeling funny, but not from his knee. He placed his crutches down beside him, then carefully lowered himself to the grass and sighed. Using crutches was hard. Diego plonked down beside him, head between his paws. Hani gave his white fur a pat.

He felt bad he hadn't agreed to help Coach, but playing for the Subway Socceroos was Hani's dream. He knew their coach, Justine Williams, had been an amazing footballer. She'd even played for the Young Matildas before deciding that the thing she enjoyed most was helping other players be the best they could. He was different. He had to stay focused.

'Okay. Everyone ready?' Coach asked.

Hani lifted his head. They'd set up in a starting formation. Sasha had the ball. He saw her quickly adjust the headband holding back her bobbed brown hair, then lean forward, ready to run. Harper and Charlie were on either side in the midfield, while Kyra and Sam were up forward. Coach had moved Ava back into defence with Kat and Luka. Meili was in goal. Finn and Crabbie were waiting to the side.

Brrrp!

Sasha slid the ball to Harper. That was normal. But what happened next had Hani sitting up straighter. Instead of hanging back, Kat raced forward. Harper passed her the ball. Kat quickly sent it wide where Charlie was flying up the sideline.

I wonder . . . Hani's eyes narrowed as he watched the play progress. Something looked different. Then it hit him.

It's a 3-3-2 formation instead of a 3-2-3.

Hani's mind started to churn.

The 3-3-2 gave more options in attack, particularly if Kat and Ava moved forward with Charlie and Harper. That made sense against Newhurst. It would, hopefully, keep Merridale in control. On the flip side, Charlie and Harper would be doing a lot of running to get back to cover the centre of the pitch when the Fever shifted to defence. Luckily they were both super fast.

Harper was dribbling now. She passed to Kyra, who was waiting near the top corner of the penalty box. Kyra moved further down the pitch as Sam raced in front of the goal. Kyra pivoted, then passed. Sam stopped the ball, then kicked it into the back corner of the net.

Hani was always impressed when he saw his team in action. Usually, it was on the sideline, waiting to be subbed on. He wanted to be out there now.

The muscles in his jaw tightened with frustration as he heard Coach's whistle.

Hani shifted, repositioning his injured left leg. Why couldn't he have hurt himself a couple of weeks later?

'Look after that leg okay, Hani,' Coach said as she jogged past on her way to the clubhouse.

'Uh, thanks Coach,' he said, confused.

Where is she going?

He looked towards his team. They were re-setting the drill, but Harper was looking at him, pointing frantically in the direction Coach had just run off.

He couldn't get comfortable, so he stood up and twisted to look behind him. His eyes opened wide. Coach was shaking hands with a woman and a man. He'd know them anywhere – CommBank Matildas star Kyah Simon and Craig Goodwin from the Subway Socceroos.

CHAPTER 3

Harper looked around the Fever Creek House. Her teammates were all talking excitedly about seeing Kyah Simon and Craig Goodwin enter the Merridale clubhouse with Coach.

'For the last time, I don't know,' Kyra said, throwing her hands in the air. 'All she said was that she had a meeting. My mum might be our coach, but she doesn't tell me *everything*.'

There were a few grumbles, but slowly

the conversation moved on to other topics.

The creek house was their special meeting place, built in the bush, across a tiny creek behind Merridale Oval. Kyra and Meili found the abandoned little building when they were in the U8s, the year Harper joined the Fever, and they'd been given permission to do it up. Even with a huge tree growing up through the middle of it, it fitted the whole team, as well as chairs and a table. Harper's favourite thing was the posters of the CommBank Matildas and Subway Socceroos. It was amazing for Harper to think how many of their football heroes the Fever had met this season. She could see them all on the wall – Joel King, Awer Mabil, Milos Degenek and Marco Tilio from the Socceroos and Mary Fowler, Emily van Egmond, Lydia

Williams, Courtney Nevin, Caitlin Foord and Kyah Simon from the Matildas. Then just today, Kyah and Craig had been at their club. Harper may have been feeling a bit down, but she knew how lucky she was.

Harper checked the time on her phone. She had to leave the creek house early. Pontswich Hill Football Academy had called. She'd been shortlisted for a scholarship and the interview was that night. Harper's hands trembled. She took a deep breath.

'We need to nail this game on Saturday,' Charlie said to the group. 'We can't let Newhurst win. They're just not nice.'

'Maybe they'll be better this year,' Ava suggested.

'What happened with these guys, anyway?' Sam asked.

Harper looked at him surprised, then remembered this was his first season with the Fever. He'd come from England. It felt like he'd been with them forever.

'They're horrible,' Sasha said, leaning forward. 'They say mean stuff when we're out on the pitch.'

'And they can be really rough,' Charlie said. 'Last year, they tripped Kyra up so many times.'

'And Harper,' Kyra added, 'remember, that girl elbowed you in the ribs so hard you had to go off.'

Harper looked down. She remembered.

'We need to stop worrying about what Newhurst *might* do,' Kat said. 'If HIP camp taught me anything, it's not to get caught up in my head.'

'Totally.' Crabbie gave Kat a fist bump.

It had been a few weeks since the whole team had taken part in the High Potential Pathway Program weekend, or HIP camp as the kids called it. Harper knew it hadn't been easy for Kat or Crabbie. Some of the other kids weren't nice to them, but they'd pulled it together. It had been awesome to watch them play alongside a few of the Matildas and Socceroos in the Game of Stars finale.

'Let's talk about Gala Day instead,' Kyra said with a smile. 'We need to come up with an activity to run for the little kids.'

'If it's even on,' Finn muttered.

'What do you mean?' Sam asked.

'Finn and I saw Old Noel when we were putting the goals away at the clubhouse,' Sasha explained. 'He said there are storms coming.'

'Big storms,' Finn added. 'Like, huge. Like, biggest-in-fifty-years huge.'

'And Noel's been at Merridale, like, forever, so he would know,' Sasha said, arms crossed.

'When?' Harper said quietly.

Sasha shrugged. 'Not sure. He said maybe this weekend, maybe early next week.'

Harper frowned.

'We could do a goal-kicking game,' Hani suggested. 'I saw this cool thing online where there were some holes cut in a big board and you got points depending on which one you kicked the ball through.'

'We could add a slot at the bottom for the really little kids,' Meili suggested. 'So it's easy for them to get points as well.'

'Massive,' Hani said. 'I love it. We've got stuff at home we could use.'

'I could come over tomorrow after school and help paint if you want,' Sasha said.

'Me too,' Finn added.

Kyra put her hand up. 'Me three.'

'What should we give as prizes?' Meili asked.

Everyone went quiet.

Harper saw a sly grin spread across Crabbie's face. 'Hani could give away some of his slushie vouchers,' he said.

'Hey!' Hani pretended to be shocked, then he smiled. 'It's not a bad idea. I do have nine, after all.'

Harper stayed quiet as her teammates started chatting in smaller groups again. This could be one of the last times she was here with her friends. Ever.

Harper's phone buzzed. She glanced down.

‘Everything okay, Harper?’ Meili asked quietly.

‘Sure,’ Harper said, blinking and putting a smile on her face. Meili raised an eyebrow.

‘I have to go,’ Harper said. ‘I’ve got an appointment.’ Her heart was hammering. It wasn’t a lie, but it wasn’t the whole truth either. Harper hated lies.

‘Okaaay,’ Meili said, but clearly she wasn’t convinced. ‘See you tomorrow?’

Harper smiled. ‘Sure.’

As she crossed the stepping stones, Harper thought again about what the goalie had said earlier. She’d asked what the Fever would do without Harper.

What am I going to do without them?

CHAPTER 4

'This is going to be so awesome,' Kyra said as she dropped her paintbrush in a jar of water.

'Yeah,' Hani said, hobbling backwards, trying to keep the weight off his sore leg. 'I can paint the numbers on when it dries.'

It was Friday afternoon and Kyra, Charlie, Sasha and Finn were at Hani's house to work on their Gala Day activity.

Hani's little sister Aisha came running into the garage holding a whistle. Two of her friends were close behind. 'Ni-ni, come and be coach for us.'

Hani smiled. This was his sister's first season with Merridale in the U6 Ravens. Hani's twin brothers were in the U8s.

'Aisha, I told you to leave your brother and his friends alone,' Hani's father said, walking in behind her. 'That's looking great,' he added.

'Thanks Mr Hasan,' Sasha replied.

'I've put some snacks out.' Mr Hasan pointed through the house to the back deck.

'Awesome, I'm starving,' Finn said with a grin.

'Thanks Dad.' Hani limped after his friends. The pain had settled overnight, but he still couldn't put much weight on his leg. What hurt more was what his mum and dad had told him when he'd arrived home from school: the scan of his knee didn't look good and he had to see a specialist. He was refusing to think about it.

'Pleeeease Hani,' Aisha said, before he had a chance to sit down. 'Just one go. Pleeeease.'

He loved his little sister, even if she could be a bit too enthusiastic about getting him to play football with her. 'Okay,' Hani said, taking the whistle. As soon as he hopped onto the grass he was surrounded by the three excited girls.

'Now remember, use the first touch to control the ball,' Hani said. 'Open up, stay balanced, and lift your leg so you can stop the ball with the inside of your foot.' He carefully lifted his sore leg, pointing to the spot. 'Also, keep your foot relaxed. What else?'

Aisha's hand shot up. 'Look up, so we can see our teammates and any defenders.'

'Right,' Hani said. The three girls spread out. 'Ready?'

They nodded.

Brrrp! Hani blew the whistle.

One of Aisha's friends nudged the ball to the third girl who had run forward. Hani smiled at the look of concentration on her face as she stopped the ball, tongue stuck out. She looked up.

'Over here, Milla,' Aisha called out. Milla kicked to Aisha, who took off dribbling.

'Remember to look up, Aisha,' Hani reminded her.

She took another step, then passed back to the first friend, who kicked the ball into the goal.

Everyone cheered and laughed as the girls ran around hugging each other as if they'd won a FIFA World Cup™ final.

Hani was still chuckling as he hobbled back up the stairs and sat down with his Fever teammates.

'You're good at that,' Kyra said, popping a grape in her mouth.

'Good at what?' he said, grabbing one of his dad's chocolate brownies.

'Helping them,' Kyra explained. 'Coaching. You should take Mum up on her offer to be her assistant this weekend.'

'Totally,' Charlie added. 'And you know so much stuff, all the different formations and things.'

Hani's smile slipped away. 'But I don't want to be a coach,' he said. 'I'm a player.'

'Yeah, of course,' Finn said. 'But while you can't play, maybe –'

'I said no!' Hani snapped. He could feel heat in his face and his heart was pounding. 'I'm *going* to play again. At Merridale, then A-League hopefully and one day, for Australia.' He looked at each of his friends. 'The same as all of you. Okay?'

Hani's fists were clenched in his lap. *Why don't they understand?*

'Uh, sure,' Finn said quietly. 'Doesn't matter. Like you said, you'll be back soon.'

The others stayed silent. No-one looked his way.

'Sorry,' Hani muttered. 'It's just . . . well, I have to see a specialist.'

Sasha frowned. 'Why?'

'You know how I mentioned that thing under my kneecap, the meniscus?' Hani asked. They nodded. 'Well, it's not right. That's why it's so sore. Discoid or something. I can't remember.' Hani hung his head, digging his nail into the timber of the table. 'I might not be allowed to play football for weeks or months maybe. Even then, it might not get better on its own.'

'Oh Hani. Hopefully it won't be that bad,' Kyra said quietly.

Hani nodded, but he still didn't look up. 'Yeah.'

The silence dragged on until Sasha cleared her throat. 'We need to lock in the Gala Day prizes,' she said. 'My dads have a few water bottles and things from the TV station they said we could use.'

Hani gave her a small smile, grateful at the change in topic.

'Were you serious about the vouchers, Hani?' Charlie asked. 'Maybe even just two or three?'

'Absolutely,' Hani said.

Kyra pulled out a notebook and jotted down ideas.

Hani knew he'd overreacted about the idea of coaching. He did enjoy helping his little sister and her friends. It always gave him such a happy feeling inside and he was often surprised at how much he knew. But he'd always wanted to play for the Subway Socceroos. Now, because of his knee, he didn't know if that dream would ever come true.

CHAPTER 5

Harper kept her eyes fixed on her football boots as she stood facing her mum and dad in the Merridale oval car park. The grey clouds matched her mood.

'I don't understand, Peanut,' her dad said. 'I would have thought you'd want your friends to know this is your last game.'

'It *may* be my last game,' Harper said.

'Harper.' She looked up and her mum gave her a gentle smile. 'There's no maybe, honey. You know that.'

'But I might not get the scholarship,' Harper said. 'Then what? You said –'

'– that we'd be going anyway.' Harper's mum sighed.

'From everything the selectors said on Thursday night, it sounds like that scholarship is pretty much in the bag,' her dad added.

Harper's face felt hot. 'I know,' she said quietly. 'I just don't want everyone to, you know, be different.' She looked at her parents, willing them to understand. 'Please. Can you not say anything yet? When we find out about the scholarship – I'll tell them then. Besides, we've still got Gala Day in a week, remember.'

Her parents shared a look, the type that had Harper convinced they could read each other's minds.

Her mum nodded. 'Okay.'

Harper let out a breath as her dad pulled her into a hug.

'Now that's settled, it's time to get your game head on,' he said. 'And even if your friends don't know, try to enjoy every minute of this game with them. Okay?'

She nodded into his chest.

'Hey Harper.' She let go of her dad as Hani limped towards her. He only had one crutch today. Even though he wasn't playing, he was still dressed in their yellow and green Merridale uniform. 'You ready?' he asked.

'You bet.' Harper pushed back her glasses and picked up her Merridale bag. She smiled at her parents. 'See you over there.'

'Check out those clouds.' Hani pointed to horizon as they walked to where their Fever teammates were setting up. 'Maybe Noel was right about those storms.'

Harper squinted into the distance. The clouds were black and blue, with swirling patterns that made them seem extra nasty.

'I hope not,' she said. 'I really don't like playing in the rain. It makes my glasses all smudgy.' She dropped her bag with the growing pile.

'I don't like the rain either,' Ava said, coming to stand with them. 'Rain equals mud, and I *really* don't like mud. Remember that game against Brolstan FC? There was mud in everything for weeks.'

Crabbie laughed. 'I *loved* that game. Bring it on, I say. Hey Diego.'

The golden retriever came bounding over, dressed for game day in his very own Merridale jersey. Number 10 – the same as legend Diego Maradona. Harper smiled as Diego tucked his furry head under Crabbie's hand, tongue flopping out the side of his mouth.

Coach was right behind. 'Okay, you lot. It's time to get moving,' she said. 'You know the drill. Off you go.'

Harper caught glimpses of Newhurst FC as they did their warm-up and stretch. Each time she did, her stomach did a little flip-flop. They were all huge. Hani-size huge. Tower-over-her huge. A Newhurst girl caught Harper staring. Harper offered a tentative smile. The girl rolled her eyes and looked away.

'Over here, Fever.' Coach waved them into a group.

'Did you see the Newhurst kids?' Crabbie said, eyes wide. 'They're so *big*. What's with that?'

'That's nothing you need to worry about, Crabbie,' Coach said. 'Play your own game. Height doesn't make them better players.'

'I read that being tall can give players an advantage in defence,' Hani said. 'But shorter players are often more agile and technical, which is especially good in attack.'

Harper smiled. She'd missed this Hani.

'Look at Lionel Messi,' Hani continued. 'He's only 170 centimetres tall and he's the GOAT. He led Argentina to win the 2022 World Cup – his *fifth* World Cup! Mind you, it was pretty cool the Socceroos got to play against them in the round of sixteen.'

Harper had watched the game with her family. She'd never forget it. Australia had lost 2–1. So close.

Hani wasn't done. 'And then what about Diego Maradona,' he said. 'He was even shorter than Messi. He was only . . .' His voice trailed off as he finally noticed his teammates' expressions. Harper did her best not to giggle. Coach had both eyebrows raised high on her forehead.

'So, yeah . . . don't worry about the tall thing,' Hani muttered.

Everyone laughed, except Hani. Harper watched him shrug. There was still something not quite Hani about Hani.

'Thanks for the pep talk, Hani,' Coach said. 'You sure you're not angling for my job?' She winked. Hani only shrugged.

Strange.

Harper tried to focus on the game plan Coach was sharing with the team, but she knew something wasn't right with her friend. She *would* find out, but for now, there was a football match to play.

*

Harper's heart was thumping as she waited for the referee to blow his whistle and start the game. Newhurst had the kick-off, so it was more important than ever that she was ready. Her opponent wasn't making it easy. Harper was sure the girl was the tallest on the team, a whole head taller, and she kept pushing her elbow against Harper's arm.

'Stay out of my way,' the girl muttered, trying to move into a better position.

Harper gritted her teeth and held her ground. She might be smaller, but she had a job to do. Crabbie was starting as goalie. She glanced his way. He looked unusually serious. They all knew this would be tough.

Brrrp!

The girl had been leaning against her to try to stop her moving, but it also gave Harper a clue about which way she would go. Harper stuck to the girl like glue as her eyes followed the ball.

Newhurst were good, but so were the Fever. While Harper blocked her opponent, she saw the other Newhurst midfielder send the ball out towards a player running down the sideline. Ava ran forward and tackled the boy. He spun, kicking the ball backwards to a Newhurst girl at the centre of the pitch. Sasha was on her straightaway.

Harper's opponent faked and tried to get around her. The girl's movements were getting rougher, and she was grunting in frustration, but Harper stayed with her. Then the ball was coming towards them. Harper knew that if she timed it right, she might be able to intercept.

Oomph.

An elbow in Harper's side knocked her just as she needed to move. It gave her a jolt but wasn't obvious enough for the referee to see. It also meant Harper missed her window to steal the ball, but she didn't give up. She raced in front of her opponent, tackling and forcing her to pass.

Harper watched the ball, waiting for another opportunity. Her teammates were defending hard, but there was something about the Newhurst kids. They weren't smiling. None of them looked like they were having fun. Luka raced forward. Harper wasn't sure how it happened, but one minute her teammate was tackling, the next he was on the ground. The Newhurst striker kicked for goal. Crabbie was in front of their goal – but he was looking at Luka.

'Crabbie!' she called out.

He looked up as the ball flew past into the back of the net.

Crabbie shook his head but was clearly more worried about his friend than the goal. Harper was too. Luka stood up slowly, rolling his ankle and nodding at something Kat said. He gave Coach a thumbs up.

As Harper jogged back to her starting position a fat raindrop landed on her head. She frowned, and not just because of the weather.

CHAPTER 6

Hani watched his soggy teammates jog off the pitch at half-time. The rain had turned their yellow jerseys a darker shade of gold. From the grim expressions on their faces, they weren't feeling any better about the game than he was watching it. He stood up and limped over to where they were huddling together under the Merridale marquee.

'I can see it's tough out there,' Coach said. 'But you're doing really well to be holding them at one-all.'

'They're just not nice, Coach,' Harper said. She was rubbing the side of her arm.

'I know.' Coach sighed. 'People handle pressure differently.' She looked around the group. 'You are all amazing players. They,' she pointed towards the Newhurst team, 'know that. You can win if you play *your* game, not theirs.'

Hani looked from Coach to his team-mates. He saw them all stand a bit straighter. Sasha even cracked a smile.

'Believe in yourselves,' Coach said gently. 'I know you don't like me saying it, but remember, it isn't whether you win or lose . . .' She paused.

'. . . it's how you play the game,' Hani recited with his teammates.

'Right. Now to the second half.' Coach

looked at her phone. 'Meili, you're on for Crabbie. Watch that striker. He comes in quickly when he gets the ball.'

Meili nodded.

'How's your ankle, Luka?' Coach asked.

'It's okay,' he said. 'I'm good to keep going.'

Coach nodded. 'Then Charlie, I want you up forward, but you two stay warm,' Coach said, looking at Finn and Crabbie. 'This drizzle looks like it's set in, so we'll be doing some subbing this half.'

'The rest of you, let's try the 3-3-2 we practised in training. It's time to show Newhurst what the Fever is made of. Hands in.'

Hani reached in with his teammates.

'FEVER TIME!' they called out, lifting their hands into the air.

‘What do you think, Hani,’ Coach said, coming to stand beside him. ‘Is 3-3-2 a good call?’

Hani didn’t want to talk about strategy, he wanted to play. He also didn’t want to be rude. ‘It’s an attacking formation,’ he said. ‘If we can control the ball, we’ve got a better chance, so it makes sense.’

He felt Coach’s eyes on him. She was smiling.

Hani pressed his lips together.

‘Are you sure you don’t want to –’

‘No,’ Hani said.

Coach raised one eyebrow, then turned back to the game.

Hani frowned and sat on the bench. His knee was aching.

Brrrp!

Sasha had the ball to start. Harper and Charlie were lined up across the midfield.

Sasha kicked to Charlie. Harper raced forward to support Kyra and Sam closer to goal. Hani was always impressed by how fast his tiny teammate was. Kat and Ava had darted towards the midfield too as planned.

'Keep the ball moving,' Hani called out.

He saw Coach glance his way. Hani kept his eyes on his teammates.

Charlie dribbled then passed to Kat near the sideline. She flicked the ball straight back to Sasha, who quickly slid it across the pitch to Harper. The Fever were passing so quickly, their Newhurst opponents were struggling to keep up.

Hani smiled as he saw Kyra racing down the side of the penalty box, just like she had in training. Harper saw it too. She passed to Kyra, who spun and sent the ball towards the centre of the box where she knew Sam was waiting. He didn't hesitate, booting the ball high into the corner of the net.

'Yes!' Hani called out.

Seconds into the second half, it was 2–1.

After the surprise attack, Newhurst re-grouped and it was back to trading ends, with no-one able to get the upper hand. As the drizzle increased to light rain, Coach subbed Finn on for Kyra, and Crabbie went out to give Ava a break in defence, while Meili stayed as goalie.

'It's brutal,' Kyra said as she wrapped a towel around her shoulders. 'But we just need to hold on.'

The ball was down Newhurst's end when Hani saw Kat slip on the wet grass. Her opponent didn't hesitate, kicking wildly towards goal.

Hani held his breath.

Meili dived and got her hands on the ball, but it was so slippery, she couldn't hold it. The ball dropped to the ground and rolled over the goal line.

Hani let out his breath. It was 2–2. The rain was coming down harder.

His teammates were jogging back to their starting positions when lightning lit up the sky. Hani had been so focused on the game, he hadn't realised how dark it had become. He counted in his head.

1–2–3–4–5–6–7–8–9–10–11–12–13 –

BOOM!

Everyone jumped as a huge clap of thunder shook the ground. Diego flattened himself on the grass.

One kilometre for every three seconds.

'That's close,' Hani said.

'Too close,' Coach replied.

The referee was already blowing his whistle, a sound being repeated around the oval. They couldn't play if the storm was closer than ten kilometres away. This one already was.

Parents and players took off for their cars or the clubhouse. Pain flared through Hani's knee as he tried to keep up with his friends. He slowed, gritting his teeth as the rain came down harder, gluing his Merridale jersey to his back. His teammates were already under cover. He limped faster, trying to find a way that didn't hurt. His eyes were stinging. He blinked quickly.

'Come on, Hani,' Harper called out.

He'd just made it to the verandah when there was another crack of thunder. Seconds later, the horizon was split by a jagged line of light. Then the sky opened, dumping the heaviest rain Hani had ever seen.

CHAPTER 7

'I can't believe it,' Harper said.

Meili shook her head. 'It's . . . it's . . .'

'It's a mess. That's what it is.' Harper turned as Old Noel walked out through the door.

It was Monday afternoon and the Fever were back at Merridale Oval. There were huge puddles, broken branches and leaves everywhere.

'You should have seen it yesterday,' Noel continued. 'The water was coming through the doors.'

'But it'll be okay by Saturday, right?' Harper asked. 'For Gala Day.'

Noel looked across the oval, arms crossed. Harper and Meili glanced at each other with identical frowns. Noel never looked this serious.

Noel sighed. 'Honestly, I don't know.'

Harper felt his words like a blow. Noel was always happy when he was at Merridale. He'd played for the club when he was a kid and as an adult. He'd even captained a team that won the Merridale Cup, the club's top prize. And when he stopped playing, he stayed around. Now, as well as cooking the barbecue and making awesome slushies, Noel kept the clubhouse running. No-one could imagine Merridale without him.

Harper was trying hard to hold it together, but if Noel couldn't be positive, then . . .

'It'll be okay, Harper,' Hani said quietly, coming to stand beside her. All her team-mates were out on the balcony now.

'Yeah,' she said, trying to smile. 'I'm just tired. I didn't sleep well with the storm and stuff.'

'Well, this isn't looking great, is it?' Coach said.

'We're still having Gala Day though, aren't we, Coach?' Kat asked.

'I don't know,' Coach said. 'I have an important meeting soon and then I'll talk with Tom. As Merridale President, he'll have the final say.'

'But Mum, Gala Day *has* to happen,' Kyra said.

Coach squeezed Kyra's shoulder. 'Just be patient.'

'If you want *any* chance of it going ahead, we'll need to get all this cleaned up,' Noel said.

'You can count on us.' Crabbie put his hand in the air. 'Just point me at the mess.'

Old Noel spun Crabbie towards the door. 'No time like the present. You lot, inside with me.' Harper heard him chuckle as he followed her through the door.

It *was* fun. Working alongside her team-mates, sweeping, mopping and cleaning the kitchen cupboards, Harper started to feel more positive.

'It's lucky you kids helped put those boxes on the shelves a while back,' Noel said as they tackled the storeroom. 'The ones on the floor have a bit of water damage. I need a couple of you to sort through them.' Noel looked straight at Hani. 'Any volunteers?'

Hani grinned.

'I'll help too,' Harper offered.

With so much chaos inside, Harper moved the damaged boxes to a tarp on the verandah. Hani slid to the ground, stretching out his leg. He looked relieved to be sitting down. He was in the best mood she'd seen him in for a while, so Harper didn't mention his knee. They started sorting the contents into two piles – to throw away and to keep.

‘Check this out,’ Hani said. ‘It’s an old coaching manual. Says here it’s from 1980.’

‘Look at the outfits.’ Harper giggled as Hani flicked through the pages. She felt lighter than she had in days. She stood up. ‘I’ll go grab a garbage bag from . . .’

Harper’s voice trailed off. She couldn’t believe what she was seeing. Kyah Simon and Craig Goodwin were back and heading their way.

‘Harper, what . . .’ Hani fell silent too. ‘Oh!’ he said.

Harper’s heart was racing.

‘Hi there,’ Kyah said. ‘We’re here to see Justine Williams.’

Harper nodded and swallowed. ‘Um, okay. She’s our coach.’

‘I’ll go tell her you’re here,’ Hani added, pulling himself up and limping into the clubhouse.

Kyah was looking out at the oval. 'You got hit hard by that storm. Should dry out quickly, though.'

Harper cleared her throat. 'I hope so,' she said quietly. 'We're meant to have our Gala Day on Saturday.'

'Gala Days are awesome,' Craig said. 'Fingers crossed for you.'

'Thanks.' Harper smiled.

'Hey guys.' Coach came out of the clubhouse with Hani right at her heels. 'Let's head to the back office,' she said. 'I see you've met Harper and Hani, two of my star midfielders.' Coach raised both eyebrows. 'I have to warn you, there are ten more excited kids inside keen to say a quick hello. I hope that's okay. I've told them we don't have long.'

'It's all good,' Craig said. 'We're always happy to chat with football-loving kids.'

'You bet,' Kyah added. 'They're what our special project is about, after all.'

'What project, Coach?' Hani asked.

Coach grinned. 'You'll have to wait and see.'

CHAPTER 8

'Do you think they're still here? Do you think we'll see Kyah Simon again?' Harper asked. 'She's incredible.'

A smile lit up Sam's face. 'Craig Goodwin is a legend too. It's insane they're here.'

'I haven't heard any cars,' Charlie said. 'So, they have to be here.'

Hani was only half listening. He was looking at the Merridale Cup in his hands.

'Excuse me, Noel,' he asked as Noel came out of the storeroom.

'Yes, Master Hani.'

'How come the Merridale Cup is always won by older teams? Why don't the kids' teams have a Cup too?'

'An interesting point, young man.' Noel helped Hani put the Cup back in its glass display cabinet. 'There's no rule that says younger teams *can't* be awarded the Cup. It's just that none ever have.'

'Maybe you kids will be the first?'

Hani spun at the sound of Kyah Simon's voice.

The rest of the team gathered around as Coach walked in with Kyah, as well as Craig Goodwin.

'I wanted to tell you all how impressive you were when you played as Half-time Heroes,' Kyah continued. 'Keep it up, okay? You guys have the perfect mix of passion, dedication and skill. Add self-belief and I have no doubt I'll see you in Australia's green-and-gold one day.'

'I second that,' Craig continued. 'Your coach told us you all went to HIP camp, so you know it can get tough. As Kyah says, self-belief is the key. Don't give up. Okay?'

Hani smiled with his teammates, all promising to keep trying hard, but inside Craig and Kyah's words made him feel sick. He didn't want to give up on his dream of playing for the Socceroos, but what if his knee became the reason he never would?

'Thanks for coming,' Hani heard Coach say as she ushered Craig and Kyah to the door. 'I think we're ready to go. Hopefully we can make the announcement . . .'

Their voices faded as they disappeared out the door.

'What announcement?' Hani asked, turning to Kyra.

'Yeah,' Sam asked. 'What's going on?'

'I told you. I don't know.' Kyra crossed her arms.

'That's right, she doesn't know,' Coach said, heading back inside. 'But I suppose I could tell you one little thing.'

Hani joined his teammates huddled around her.

Coach leaned in. 'I can tell you that . . . you're going to love it!'

Her statement was met by a chorus of groans.

'That's not fair,' Kyra said.

'That's not *anything*,' Sasha added.

'Sorry,' Coach said, grinning. 'It has to stay a secret for now.'

'Okay, everyone,' Noel said. 'Back to work!'

CHAPTER 9

Harper felt all mixed up as her mum pulled into the Merridale car park on Thursday. Merridale's Club President, Tom, had wanted to cancel Gala Day. Coach had convinced him to hold off, and he had promised to give his final decision today. Harper wanted so badly to play again with her team but she also thought it might be easier to just leave – saying goodbye was too hard.

'I wonder if Kyah Simon will be here again?' Harper's mum switched off the car.

'I doubt it,' Harper said. 'But it was *so* incredible to talk to her even once. I can't believe she remembered us from when we were Half-time Heroes!'

The thought made Harper smile.

'There it is,' her mum said, watching her. 'I've missed happy Harper.'

Harper took a drink from her water bottle.

'Well, I have some big news I hope will also make you smile,' her mum continued. 'We heard back from Pontswich Hill Football Academy.'

Harper's stomach dropped like the time she'd gone on a really big rollercoaster. She gripped her water bottle tighter. 'And?' she asked quietly.

'Honey, you've been awarded a full football scholarship. You start in three weeks.'

Harper's mouth opened and closed a few times. No words came out.

'So, now you know for sure, you can finally tell your friends,' her mum said. 'Isn't that great?'

No, no, no, no, no.

'Harper, are you okay?'

Harper nodded. She didn't want to talk. She needed to get out of the car. She needed to think. She saw Finn and Charlie run past the Merridale clubhouse door, Sasha right on their heels. The others were probably inside too.

'I need to go,' she said.

Harper's mum looked at her a moment. 'Okay, honey. Just think about it,' she said gently. 'You'd want to know if it was one of them leaving.'

Harper forced herself to walk calmly to the edge of the clubhouse and around the corner. When she was out of sight of the car park and her mum, Harper slid to the ground. Leaning against the wall, she let tears roll down her cheeks. She was out of excuses, but she *still* didn't want to tell her friends.

I don't want it to be real.

'I think that's a great suggestion to start us off.'

'And they're a perfect match too.'

Harper leaned back against the wall. The voices were Coach and Kyah Simon and they were getting closer. Maybe they wouldn't notice her.

'Hello Harper,' Coach said.

Harper looked up slowly.

'Harper, what's wrong?' Coach crouched down quickly beside her. 'Has something happened?'

Harper shook her head, not trusting herself to speak.

'I thought you'd be bubbling with excitement.' Coach stroked her shoulder. 'It's not every day you get accepted into one of the best football schools in Australia!' Coach stood up. 'Kyah and I were just talking about your scholarship.'

Harper's mouth dropped open.

How did Coach know?

Coach smiled. 'Who do you think wrote the letter supporting your application?'

'Harper, that's seriously impressive,' Kyah said. 'That's a tough school to get into. Your teammates must be proud.'

Harper looked at her feet, her eyes stinging. 'Actually, I haven't told them.' She blinked and swallowed.

They all turned at the sound of yelling and laughing inside the clubhouse.

'Harper, will you be okay if I leave you with Kyah for a moment?' Coach asked, handing Harper a tissue. 'I think I need to check what's going on inside. Craig should be here soon too.'

Harper wiped her nose and nodded.

'I'll bring Craig to the meeting room when he gets here,' Kyah said.

As Harper watched Coach disappear, Kyah slid down to sit beside her.

'Why haven't you told your teammates?' Kyah asked.

Harper shrugged. 'I'm worried everything will change. I don't want to lose my friends.'

'You won't lose them. Want to know why?'

Harper nodded. A tear trickled down her cheek.

'You'll always be part of the Merridale Fever,' Kyah said. 'I've been on so many incredible teams, Harper. Club teams as a kid, W-League teams, international teams

and of course, the Matildas. Every person I've played with stays connected to me, because we've worked hard together on and off the pitch and we love the same thing – football.'

Kyah stood up.

'Try to think of how you'd feel if you were in their shoes. Wouldn't you want to celebrate every moment left that you could?'

Harper nodded. She could see now that her mum and Kyah were right.

'You Fever kids have a special bond,' Kyah continued. 'You'll never lose that. I promise.'

'Thanks Kyah,' Harper said as she stood up too. 'You're right. I'm going to tell them today.'

CHAPTER 10

'Try not to worry about what the specialist told you,' Hani's dad said as they arrived at Merridale oval. 'If resting doesn't help, we can consider the knee surgery. It'll be okay.'

'Yeah. I guess.'

Hani knew his dad meant well. But *months* of taking it easy to settle his knee down, like the specialist said, definitely wasn't okay. Not when he wanted to try out for reps and there was summer football and so many other things. He opened the car door.

'Isn't that Craig Goodwin?' Hani's dad pointed to a car that had pulled up near them. Craig noticed Hani and waved.

'I gotta go. Bye Dad,' Hani said. He winced as he climbed out of the car, the quick movement sending pain shooting into his knee. The compression bandage was helping, but it didn't stop all the pain. At least he wasn't on crutches anymore.

'That looks sore,' Craig said, pausing near the front of his car.

'Yeah,' Hani said, 'it is.'

'What did you do?' Craig asked.

'I twisted it, but apparently I have a discoid meniscus,' Hani explained.

'That doesn't sound like fun,' Craig said as they walked towards the clubhouse.

'Nah. I also just found out I have to rest it. Maybe for months.' Hani frowned. 'Not good timing.'

'Is there ever a good time to be injured?' Craig said. 'I had a groin injury in the middle of 2022. I had to miss some big games. That was hard. But resting meant I was fit to be picked for the Socceroos World Cup Squad.'

'And you were awesome,' Hani said. 'You scored a goal and everything.'

'Yeah, it was pretty cool,' Craig agreed.

'It was more than cool,' Hani said. 'It was massive!'

Caught up in the memory, Craig and Hani grinned at each other. Then Hani's face dropped.

'It's hard not knowing when I'll be back,' he admitted quietly.

'No doubt. But you can still be part of everything by coming along, like you're doing today. It's nice you're here to support your team,' Craig said. He glanced down. 'What have you got there?'

Hani looked down too. He'd forgotten he was holding the water-damaged coaching book he'd found when they cleaned up the clubhouse. Hani had slid it into his bag when Harper wasn't looking. He didn't want to admit it, but he'd found it really interesting.

'Hey, cool,' Craig said. 'Can I take a look?'

'There's a drill I thought could be good for our team,' Hani said tentatively as Craig flicked through the book. 'It's a bit old, so I made some notes.' He pointed at a sticky note stuck inside.

Craig stayed quiet reading. Hani wasn't prepared to say he would help coach, but he was secretly proud of what he'd done. He hoped Craig thought it was okay.

Craig closed the book and handed it back. 'That's impressive,' he said. Hani felt huge relief. 'I like how you adapted the drill. You might be a good candidate for the new mentor program I've been working on with your coach. We're just meeting to finalise the details today.'

'No thanks,' Hani said quickly. 'I just want to play.' He felt heat in his cheeks. 'I want to represent Australia one day, maybe even at a World Cup like you. I can't get distracted.'

'That's a good goal,' Craig said as they reached the clubhouse. 'You know, with hard work, you can do anything you set your mind to,' he added. 'But also look for the value in different experiences. Learning about coaching or at least helping other players could make *you* an even better player one day.'

'Yeah,' Hani said. He hadn't thought about it that way, but it kind of made sense. 'Thanks.'

Hani turned to see Harper walking around the corner – with Kyah Simon. Harper's eyes looked a bit red, like she'd been crying, but she had a smile on her face.

'Hi Craig,' Kyah said. 'Justine's meeting us in the office.'

‘Great.’ Craig turned to Hani. ‘See you later, and think about what I said.’

Harper and Hani waved as Kyah and Craig walked off chatting. As Harper turned to face him, Hani noticed her red eyes again.

‘Are you okay, Harper?’ he asked.

‘I wasn’t,’ she admitted. ‘But I think I am now.’

*

Coach had called them all out onto the verandah.

‘I know you want to hear our decision about Gala Day,’ Coach said. ‘But first, Harper has something she’d like to share.’

Hani watched Harper. She looked more nervous than sad.

‘This is so hard,’ Harper said. ‘I probably should have told you earlier, but I didn’t know how.’

Hani saw Coach give Harper an encouraging smile.

Harper looked around at everyone, then spoke in a rush. 'I'm-leaving-Merridale-we're-moving-to-Pontswich-Hill-and-I've-been-offered-a-scholarship-at-the-football-academy.'

It took a moment for Hani to process her words. Then it hit him.

Harper's leaving.

Hani felt weird – sad and happy at the same time. He would miss Harper, but getting into Pontswich Hill was massive.

'OMG. That's so exciting,' Meili said, when everyone had settled a bit. 'But we'll miss you.'

'It's totally awesome,' Crabbie agreed. 'And it gives us a good excuse for a road trip to the country to visit.'

Hani thought about her tears, then his

stomach dropped. 'When are you leaving?' he asked.

'In just over a week. After the end-of-season barbecue,' Harper said. 'I'm sorry I didn't tell you all sooner.'

'Well, we know now,' Kyra said. 'And it's extra motivation to beat Newhurst at Gala Day. Assuming they come.'

'And assuming it's on,' Meili reminded her.

The Fever turned as one to look at Coach. She smiled.

'You'll have your celebration, kids. Gala Day is a go!'

CHAPTER 11

Harper stretched her arms above her head. It was six-thirty, and they were already at Merridale Oval. Gala Day didn't officially start until eight-thirty, but her mum said Coach had messaged to ask them to come early. She'd assumed it was the whole team, but she hadn't spotted anyone else yet.

Harper didn't mind the early start. She'd slept better than she had for weeks, and was happy and ready to go. It was already hard to remember why she'd been so worried about telling her teammates.

'There she is,' her mum said, pointing towards the clubhouse.

Harper's hands started to tremble.

Coach wasn't alone. There was a camera, a cameraman, a man wearing a Football Australia jacket and a woman with a brown ponytail. Harper couldn't see her face.

'Mum, what's going on?' Harper asked as they walked towards the group.

'Coach asked if you could do an interview about the scholarship,' her mum said. 'That's all I know.'

'Thanks for the warning,' Harper mumbled.

'Here she is.' Coach held her arms out as Harper walked up.

'Hi Coach.'

'This is Luke from Football Australia,' Coach said. 'And this . . .' The other woman turned around. '. . . is Kyra.'

Harper tried not to stare. First Kyah Simon and now Kyra Cooney-Cross, the CommBank Matildas' rising midfield star. This was the best week ever.

'Hi Harper,' Kyra said.

'Harper,' Luke said. 'I'm excited to tell you that you've been chosen as the first spotlight player in our Rising Stars Mentor Program.'

Harper looked at Coach.

'You know all those meetings I've been having?' Coach asked.

Harper nodded.

'I've been working with Football Australia to get this program off the ground,' Coach explained. 'It's like a buddy system for football kids.'

Luke nodded. 'At club level, we'll be matching older kids with those starting out, and then when you reach Under 12s you'll be eligible to be paired with some of the country's best players.'

'Like you and Kyra,' Coach said with a smile. 'We think you'll make a great team.'

'I agree,' Kyra said. 'I'm so excited about this, Harper. I think I'm going to learn lots from you too.'

Harper looked around. Everyone was grinning at her. 'Umm . . . wow. Thank you. I don't know what to say.'

'You'll need to think of something,' Luke said with a laugh. 'As our first pairing, we'd like you to do a quick interview together that we can use to spread the word. Is that okay?'

'Uh, sure,' Harper said. Her stomach was doing somersaults as the cameraman set up the shot.

'Feeling okay?' Kyra asked.

'Nervous,' Harper admitted.

'Me too.'

Harper looked at her, surprised. 'But you must have done stuff like this a million times.'

'I don't know about a million,' Kyra said. 'I don't like the spotlight much. No matter how many interviews I do, I'm never sure I'm going to say the right thing. I guess it's the expectation that gets to me.'

'What do you think they want us to say now?' Harper asked.

'I don't know. But I can tell you how I approach it if you like?'

'Yes please,' Harper said.

'Just be yourself.' Kyra smiled, twisting her brown hair into a low bun. 'I know it's easy to say, but at least then, no matter what happens, you know you've done the best you can. That applies on and off the pitch.' Kyra leaned towards Harper. 'And remember, it's okay to be nervous.'

Harper already liked Kyra, a lot.

'We're ready for you,' Luke called out.

Kyra and Harper grinned at each other. 'Let's do this,' Harper said.

*

By the time the interview was finished, they had quite an audience. All her teammates had arrived, along with their families, and plenty of kids in other club jerseys. Kyra was mobbed with requests for autographs, but she promised she'd be in touch with Harper soon. Harper felt on top of the world. Not even seeing the Newhurst kids in the crowd could dampen her mood.

'Then at the end they asked me why I loved football so much,' Harper told her

teammates. They'd begged her for a second-by-second replay of the whole thing.

'What did you say?' Ava asked.

'I said there were lots of things, but one of the biggest was you guys, my team.'

Her teammates were all grinning at her. There was so much she loved about football, but these friends were number one.

‘Welcome to Merridale,’ Coach called out. She was standing in front of the clubhouse verandah. ‘Thank you for coming, even if it was touch and go.’

There was loud clapping and cheering.

Excited murmurs surrounded Harper as Coach called out the instructions for the round robin and presentation at the end of the day. Harper could hardly believe it. After all the worries and the rain, it was finally happening. She was getting to enjoy her last day playing with the Fever. As Harper ran over to get ready, her heart was so full of happiness, she thought she might burst.

CHAPTER 12

'Come on. Give it another try.' Hani smiled encouragingly at the little boy lined up at their goal-shooting game. He was perched on the edge of a padded box they'd used to mark the starting point, resting his knee.

The boy took a deep breath and then kicked. Everyone cheered as the ball slipped through one of the lower holes.

'Awesome,' Hani said clapping. 'I knew you could do it.'

‘Come and choose your prize.’ Harper called the boy over to where she had a box of football-themed things. He chose a pencil with a rubber shaped like a football on the end.

‘Me next!’ Finn’s little brother, Xavier, was at the front of the line.

‘Enjoying Gala Day, Xav?’ Hani asked.

‘You bet! I’ve been to everything. Now I just need to win a slushie.’

Xavier’s long hair had been sprayed yellow and green, he had a football painted on his cheek and he was holding a huge stick of fairy floss.

‘Okay, Xav,’ Hani said. ‘Let’s see what you can do.’

Harper rolled him a football.

Xavier handed his fairy floss to a friend and lined up in front of the board.

'Which one do I need for a slushie?' he asked.

'Either of the bottom corner holes,' Hani said. 'The ones right on the edges. They're usually the hardest balls for goal-keepers to save.'

'You've got this, Xav,' Finn said, giving his brother a pat on the back.

Xavier took a step back and kicked. The ball slipped straight through the hole on the left side of the board.

'Very nice,' Harper said.

'And you have your slushie,' Hani added, handing him a slip of paper. 'Give this to Old Noel.'

There was lots of laughter as the rest of Xavier's teammates each took their turn.

'I know you don't like me saying it, Hani,' Kyra said, 'but you're good at this.'

She licked her chocolate-covered soft serve with sprinkles and a flake.

'It's okay,' he said. 'I do kind of enjoy it. I am keen to get back kicking, though.'

'I can't believe we have to play Newhurst again,' Charlie said, jumping up on the box beside Hani.

'They weren't too bad earlier,' Meili said.

'Yeah, but they weren't too good either,' Crabbie pointed out. 'They just seem so . . . I don't know.'

'Cranky?' Sam suggested. 'I totally get what you were talking about now.'

The round robin was over. Merridale and Newhurst had both won three games and drawn against each other – that meant they were tied at the top of the table and would face up one more time in the U11s Gala Day Championship play-off.

'You know what Coach always tells us,' Hani said, 'play *our* game, not theirs.' He looked at his watch. 'Ooh, you guys better get moving. I'll pack this up.'

'Thanks Hani,' Harper said.

Please let it be a good game, he thought as he watched his teammates head to the oval. *For Harper.*

'Excuse me. Can I have a go?'

'I'm just packing up,' Hani said. 'I don't . . .' He turned to see a tiny girl wearing a Newhurst FC jersey.

'That's okay,' she said quietly. She turned as an older Newhurst girl jogged up. Hani recognised her from their rival Under 11s team. They had to be sisters.

'It's already finished,' the younger girl said.

'Wait.' Hani called out. 'You can have a go.'

The older girl looked surprised.

'It's my first Gala Day,' the younger girl said, bouncing back to his side. 'I'm going to be a striker one day, like Kyra.'

'Kyra Cooney-Cross?' Hani asked. 'But she's in the midfield.'

The girl shook her head. 'No, *your* Kyra, from Merridale Fever. I've watched every game you've played against my sister. This is her. Her name's Cassi.' She pointed at the other girl, all traces of shyness gone. 'My name's Kyra too.'

'Well, Kyra,' Hani said, 'let's see what you can do.'

Little Kyra struggled with her first two kicks. Hani could see she was getting frustrated.

'I want you to take a deep breath,' Hani said, carefully bending down beside her. 'Look where you want it to go, keep your eye on the ball, and aim right in the middle of it when you kick.'

'And I need to keep my body straight,' Kyra added.

'That's right. Okay, Kyra, you've got this.'

The next ball went right through a hole in the middle.

'I did it,' she squealed. 'Did you see, Cassi?'

The older girl smiled. Kyra technically hadn't won a slushie, but she'd tried so hard, Hani gave her a voucher anyway, and a football pencil.

'Thank you!' Kyra said, then raced off.

Cassi was still standing there. 'It's cool you let her have a go.'

Hani shrugged and smiled. 'She reminds me of my little sister. Fun and maybe a little bit crazy.'

'Yep, that's Kyra.' Cassi laughed. 'You're nice.'

Hani shrugged.

'Your teammates seem okay too.'

'They are,' Hani said.

'We thought you weren't, you know.' Cassi tilted her head.

Hani's eyebrows shot up. 'Why?'

'You're always winning,' she said.

'But not against you,' Hani reminded her. 'We always draw.'

'True,' Cassi said with a sly grin. 'I guess we'll just have to beat you guys in the final.'

'Ha!' A grin spread across Hani's face too. 'Good luck with that.'

CHAPTER 13

Harper kept reminding herself to breathe, but this was her last game with the Fever – no amount of breathing would take the big feelings away.

Hani had explained about the Newhurst girl, Cassi, and her idea that it was the Fever who weren't going to be nice. It all seemed so silly, but Harper hoped it meant this game would be fun.

'This is it,' Coach said, calling them into a circle. Harper gave Diego a pat as he sat proudly in the middle. 'The Gala Day final and more importantly, Harper's last game.' Harper lowered her eyes and stroked Diego's soft head. 'Although definitely not the last time we'll see her,' Coach added. 'Harper, any special requests?'

She pushed back her glasses. 'Um, I'd like us to win, please.'

Coach laughed. 'Right, then. That's the aim.' She crouched down. 'Remember, the halves are short, so you need to move fast and score quickly.' She looked around the circle. 'You know your positions. Meili, you'll start in goal. Crabbie, you'll get the second half. Charlie, you're off too, but you'll be going on early, so stay warm. Hands in.'

Harper put her hand in first, feeling the weight of all her teammates' hands on top.

She took a deep breath and swung her arm into the air.

'FEVER TIME!' she called out as loudly as she could.

The adrenalin kicked in as Harper jogged onto the pitch and up to her opponent.

'Hey,' the girl said, giving Harper a small smile.

Harper blinked in surprise. It was the same girl from the storm day and their earlier round robin match. She'd only ever grumbled before, but now it seemed she *was* trying to be friendly. Harper decided to be positive.

'Hello,' she said. 'I'm Harper.'

'I'm Zoe,' the girl replied. 'You're the one that's leaving, right?'

Harper nodded, surprised she knew.

Her opponent's smile got bigger. 'You know that doesn't mean I'm going easy on you, right?'

'I certainly hope not.' Harper grinned back as they turned to face the centre of the pitch. Sasha was standing ready for kick-off.

Brrrp!

Harper darted forward as Sasha slid her the ball. Her opponent, Zoe, was on her quickly. Harper used an outside touch to duck around as Kat ran up the sideline. Harper passed, keeping her body between her opponent and her teammate, giving Kat time to receive the ball. Kat dribbled towards goal then passed to Finn, but his opponent was straight on him.

Come on, Finn.

He smiled, then used a Cruyff turn to spin away from his defender. Kyra and

Sam were both in position, right near the penalty box, but were struggling to get clear. Harper was too far away to help but she saw Ava running through the midfield. Finn saw her too and kicked hard her way. Harper frowned as a Newhurst boy came out of nowhere, intercepting the ball. He sent it quickly to another boy, who turned and raced away.

The Newhurst attacker hadn't made it far before he was tackled by Sasha. He looked flustered. He had no-one to pass to with all the Fever players glued to their opponents. Then suddenly Sasha had the ball again and she needed help.

Harper faked then sprinted forward.

'Sasha, here,' she called out.

Taken by surprise, Harper's opponent was a few steps behind. Sasha slid her the ball and Harper took off. She could hear Zoe breathing just over her shoulder. Harper put on an extra burst of speed. She'd made it all the way to the side of the penalty box when she saw Kyra out of the corner of her eye. Harper stopped, spun and kicked hard and low. She held her breath as the football slid to a stop at Kyra's boot. Kyra didn't hesitate, kicking straight at goal. The goalie dived. The ball slipped past her fingers and into the back of the net.

Harper's cheeks were hurting from smiling as she headed back to the midfield to re-set.

'Nice assist,' Zoe said.

'Nice defence,' Harper replied.

She liked this version of Newhurst FC. Looking around, Harper could see she wasn't the only one feeling the change. The goalie gave Kyra a thumbs up and *everyone* was smiling, despite it being the Fever that had scored.

Harper saw the referee raise the whistle to her lips. Harper tensed her body, ready to run.

CHAPTER 14

The Fever held on to the lead until a minute before half-time, when Cassi found the back of the net for Newhurst.

'You're all doing so well,' Coach said in the break. 'You have ten more minutes to wrap things up.'

'That was such a great first half,' Meili said, surprise clear in her voice. 'The Newhurst forwards are silly. You're going to love it in goal, Crabbie.'

'My opponent is being really nice too,' Finn said. 'You were right, Hani.'

‘It happens occasionally.’ Everyone laughed.

‘Speaking of being right, how about you share your second-half idea, Hani?’ Coach asked.

Hani looked at his feet. It was one thing to tell Coach . . .

Look for the value in different experiences. That’s what Craig had said.

He glanced up and Harper gave him an encouraging smile.

‘I think we should try a 3-1-3-1 formation.’ Hani unfolded a piece of paper. ‘It’s going to give us more attacking power and solid defence. But Sasha, there’ll be a big load on you in the midfield.’

‘I can do it,’ Sasha said.

Hani nodded, pointing at the paper. ‘Sam, you’ll hang back near goal. Harper, Kyra and Charlie, you’ll be concentrating on the area here, closer to the midline. Kat, Luka and Ava, you're in defence as usual and Crabbie's in goal.'

Everyone was crowding around, nodding.

'Maybe don't start in those positions,' Hani continued. 'Newhurst has the kick-off, so this will be a surprise when we get the ball. Harper, you start near Sasha around the midfield line. We need to try to steal the ball. Once we have it, you know what to do.' Hani glanced at Coach. 'Anything else?'

'I like it,' Coach said. 'Let's get this done.'

Hani chewed his lip as he watched his teammates get into position on the pitch.

'Great plan, Hani,' Meili said. 'We'll have to try it when you're back too.'

Hani nodded. 'For sure.'

Brrrp!

Newhurst came out firing. With just three quick passes, they were already close to goal. But Kat, Luka and Ava were defending hard, forcing Newhurst to pass again and again.

Frustrated, a boy kicked towards the net.

Hani held his breath, then let it out with a whoosh as Crabbie scooped up the ball. He didn't pause, throwing the football straight to Kat. She passed to Luka, who dribbled, then sent the ball on to Ava. Hani saw Harper sprinting past the midline towards goal, while Sasha stayed around the middle of the pitch.

Hani's heart was racing.

Please let this work.

Ava's opponent wasn't giving her any space. Ava faked then cut the ball past her defender. Breaking clear, she kicked to

Charlie, who passed straight to Kyra. She stopped the ball, but her defender was right there. Hani could see her looking around. She needed help. Kyra passed as Sam darted out of the penalty box, not far from the goal line. Then suddenly a Newhurst player came sprinting past, stealing the ball. He was moving so fast, he couldn't get the football under control. The boy ran straight over the goal line.

It was the Fever's ball.

This is a chance.

Hani took a deep breath.

Charlie had the corner, but the pause had given Newhurst time to re-group. Hani could see frustration on Sam and Kyra's faces as they tried to break clear.

Suddenly Hani spotted Harper sprinting through the middle of the penalty box. Hani stood up, ignoring the pain in his knee. Charlie saw Harper too. He kicked hard. Harper didn't miss a step as she stopped the ball.

'Shoot, Harper, shoot!' Hani jumped up and down and immediately regretted it.

She kicked towards goal.

'Yes!' Hani yelled as the ball slipped into the corner of the net.

Harper had put the Fever 2–1 up. Now they just had to hold on.

*

'That was awesome,' Crabbie said, flopping back on the grass.

Hani couldn't believe the day was almost over as he sat finishing a slushie with his teammates. They all wore Gala Day Age Champion medals around their necks and huge smiles on their faces. After Harper's goal, the Fever *had* held on and won. The Newhurst kids were good sports, promising to be back fighting harder next year.

'Is everyone still coming to the presentation barbecue on Friday?' Kyra asked. 'Mum told me to check.'

There were nods all around.

'We leave on Sunday,' Harper said. 'But I wouldn't miss it for the world.'

'Shall we visit the creek house too?' Hani suggested.

Harper smiled. 'Perfect.'

CHAPTER 15

Harper's emotions were all over the place as she sat on the timber floor of the Merridale clubhouse. The room was filled with the excited voices of all the MiniRoos kids, their families and the smell of Old Noel's sausages. Her stomach growled in anticipation.

It felt like hardly any time had passed since the start-of-season barbecue where they'd met Mary Fowler from the CommBank Matildas and Joel King from the Subway Socceroos. But so much had changed.

'Thank you for coming,' Coach said to the crowd. Behind her was a table overflowing with ribbons and trophies.

'I know you're hungry, but we have a lot of awards to give out,' she said. 'And as is our tradition here at Merridale, we also have a special message for you.'

Harper looked sideways at Kyra. She shrugged.

'Lights, please,' Coach said.

The Football Australia logo appeared on the screen in front of them, followed by a very familiar face in a green-and-gold jersey.

Harper sucked in an excited breath.

'Hi everyone. My name's Garang Kuol, I'm a forward for the Subway Socceroos and I'm stoked to be sending you this video from my new club overseas.'

'Did you see him at the World Cup in Qatar?' Hani whispered, leaning close to Harper. 'Insane.'

'Yeah, but shh,' Harper said.

'Some of you probably saw me play at the 2022 FIFA World Cup™,' Garang continued. Harper looked across at Hani. They grinned. 'It was such an honour to

become the youngest person to play in a knockout round since Pelé in 1958. To come up against Argentina's legend Lionel Messi on the pitch as well – that was just unreal. I could say a dream.'

Playing for Australia. That was Harper's dream. She was going to do everything she could to make it happen, even if that meant taking the scary step of leaving the Fever.

'You guys aren't much younger than I was at that World Cup,' Garang said. 'So, my advice? Work hard, embrace every opportunity and believe in yourself – because I'm proof that anything is possible.' He grinned, the smile lighting up his face. 'Perhaps I'll be lining up beside some of you in Australia's green-and-gold one day too.'

Garang waved and the picture dissolved back into the Football Australia logo.

Cheers filled the hall as the lights came back on.

'Garang is quite remarkable,' Coach said. 'But so are you. Congratulations to all of you for an exceptional season of MiniRoos. We're going to call you up team by team to get your medals, then we have our other club prizes to give out.'

Coach started with the youngest and worked her way through the age groups. Harper cheered with her Fever teammates as kids they knew were called out – Hani's sister, Aisha, then his twin brothers, and Finn's brother, Xavier. Finally, it was the Fever's turn. One by one, Coach called out their names – Ava, Kyra, Sam, Charlie, Finn, Hani, Crabbie, Meili, Sasha, Kat and Luka. Just one to go: Harper. Her eyes prickled as Coach hung the medal around her neck, but she blinked hard.

She'd promised herself tonight would be about smiles.

'Now it's time for our club trophies,' Coach said. 'The Best and Fairest awards for each age group are decided by your coaches.'

Harper was thrilled when Xavier was awarded Best and Fairest in the Under 8s. Judging by the cheering, it was a popular choice with his teammates too.

'Now to my team,' Coach said. 'The Under 11s Merridale Fever. The person receiving this award is someone who has consistently given their all in every game they've played. Not just this year, but every season they've been with the club. They are dedicated in training, show kindness and compassion to their teammates and opponents, but never lose their fighting spirit.'

Coach smiled down at her team.

'The U11s Best and Fairest award this year goes to Harper Brown.'

Harper was sure her cheeks were bright red as she walked up to the front of the room. The Fever were on their feet, whooping and cheering. She smiled at her parents standing at the back of the hall.

'Thank you, Coach,' Harper said quietly.

'Thank *you*, Harper,' Coach replied. 'It has been such an honour. But remember, this isn't goodbye. Okay?'

Harper's eyes were blurry with tears.

I'm not going to cry, she reminded herself.

Harper forced a shaky smile as she sat back down with her teammates.

'We have one more award to give out,' Coach said.

Harper could see her teammates glancing at each other, identical looks of confusion on their faces. Usually, the Best and Fairest awards were the end of the presentation.

'As many of you know, the Merridale Cup isn't given out every year,' Coach said. 'To receive this award, teams must be nominated, then approved by the Merridale Football Club Committee.' She looked towards the clubhouse door. 'Noel, could you please come and join us?'

Noel crossed to stand beside Coach. She handed him the Cup.

'Noel's team was awarded the cup in 1970,' Coach continued. 'We thought it would be nice for him to present it today.'

Harper and Hani looked at each other again. Hani raised his eyebrows.

'It would be my pleasure,' Noel said.

'For those who don't know, the Merridale Cup isn't an award for just how well a team plays,' Coach explained.

'It's also for how much a whole team gives to this club and to football. It's never been awarded to a MiniRoos team before.'

Suddenly Harper's whole body was tingling with anticipation.

Coach grinned down at her team. 'It is with enormous pride I announce the team awarded the Merridale Cup is the Under 11s Merridale Fever.'

It felt like a dream as Harper joined her team up the front. Somehow, she ended up in the middle, her team crowded around and the Merridale Cup in her hands. As the room filled with cheers, she raised it high above her head.

CHAPTER 16

'You better watch out, Harper,' Hani said. He could see Diego creeping closer to her half-finished sausage sandwich.

The golden retriever had been glued to Harper ever since they crossed the creek and headed to the Fever Creek House. It was like he knew something was going on.

'It's okay,' Harper said. 'Here you go, Diego.'

Diego rolled his eyes as he chomped the

sandwich down, then turned his attention to Kyra.

'No chance,' Kyra said, popping the last bit of her sausage in her mouth. 'But I do love you, crazy dog.'

Diego's tongue flopped out the side, his mouth open in a grin.

'Are you all packed up?' Hani asked Harper.

'Yep,' she said. 'I'm going to really miss you guys, but it *is* starting to get exciting.'

'Totally. And you'll be playing *so* much football,' Crabbie said. 'Will there be cows and stuff where you're living?'

Harper shook her head. 'No, we're in town. But it's a small place with lots of open space around it. I'm looking forward to that.'

'We're doing a road trip to see more of Australia over the Christmas holidays,'

Sam told her. 'Mum said we might be able to visit.'

Harper smiled. 'Awesome.'

'And you'll have to send us videos about what you learn,' Meili said. 'And what you're doing with Kyra Cooney-Cross in that mentor program.'

'For sure,' Harper said. 'She called me yesterday and we've set up our first Zoom chat for next week. I'll message you all as much as I can. You'll have to keep me updated on what you're all doing as well. Especially how you're going with your knee, Hani.'

Hani had finally shared what the specialist had said. His teammates were disappointed for him but straightaway started suggesting all the football-related things he could still do.

'Speaking of messages,' Hani said, 'how cool was that video from Garang Kuol.'

'Imagine if some of us did make it to a World Cup one day,' Finn said. 'It could be us sending a message back to Merridale.'

'Not *if*.' Sasha elbowed Finn. 'When!' She smiled and looked around. 'It *is* possible, you know.'

'Absolutely,' Hani agreed. 'Sitting right here could be six future members of the CommBank Matildas and six Subway Socceroos.'

'Can you believe we're in Under 12s next year?' Ava said quietly.

'No,' Kat replied. 'I've decided to do the girls comp as well as the mixed.'

'Me too,' Kyra said. 'Plus, there's rep tryouts.'

'And don't forget summer football,' Charlie added.

'It's going to be hard to top this year, though,' Crabbie said, unusually serious. 'I mean, playing at a Socceroos match, HIP camp and now the Merridale Cup. I mean, wow.'

They all fell silent again.

'We need a photo,' Kyra said, jumping up. 'We can take a group selfie.'

Meili pulled out her phone. 'Hani, you've got the longest arms,' she said. 'Can you take it?'

'Sure,' he replied.

Hani limped forward as his teammates squashed up into a group around him. Harper was right in the front, with Diego at her feet.

The whole team. Together.

'Ready?' Hani asked. He stretched the phone out in front. 'One. Two. Three.'

'FEVER!' they yelled together.

Hani clicked the button. Football friends forever.

FOOTBALL FEVER

THE MERRIDALE FEVER

Kyra Williams

Sam Elrick

Sasha Parry

Finn Sadler

Charles 'Crabbie' Cannon

Katarina 'Kat' Horvat

Harper Brown

Hani Hasan

Meili Chen

Luka Horvat

Ava Trent

Charlie Robertson

ABOUT THE AUTHOR

Kristin Darell has been a passionate storyteller since she was a child. Whether it was making up adventures with her twin sister, or writing about the world around her, she was rarely found without a pen and paper in hand. As an adult, she made this passion her life. She worked as a broadcast news and sports journalist for major Australian news organisations for more than twenty years.

After the birth of her two children, Kristin re-focused her attention on writing for children. As an author, she has contributed to children's writing anthologies. Football Fever is her debut junior fiction series.

Kristin is a strong advocate for children's literature, working as the Program Manager for the Australian Children's Laureate Foundation. She lives on Sydney's northern beaches with her husband, two children, two dogs, pet snake and three-legged pygmy bearded dragon.

FOLLOW THE COMMBANK MATILDAS

CommBank
MATILDAS

matildas.com.au

matildas

matildas

TheMatildas

footballaustralia